IN MEMORY OF:

Helen Susie Dickman

PRESENTED BY:

The Director & Staff
of the
Brumback Library

Hamburger Heaven

Wong Herbert Yee

Houghton Mifflin Company
Boston

The text of this book is set in 16-point Versailles.
The illustrations are watercolor, reproduced in full color.

Library of Congress Cataloging-in-Publication Data

Yee, Wong Herbert.
    Hamburger Heaven / written and illustrated by Wong Herbert Yee.
       p.   cm.
    Summary: When Pinky Pig's job at Hamburger Heaven is threatened,
she launches a campaign to make the restaurant more popular with the
other animals.
    RNF ISBN 0-395-87548-X   PAP ISBN 0-618-54885-8
    [1. Hamburgers—Fiction. 2. Food habits—Fiction. 3. Restaurants—
Fiction. 4. Pigs—Fiction. 5. Animals—Fiction. 6. Stories in rhyme.] I. Title.
PZ8.3.Y42Ham   1999
[E]—dc21   98-11910   CIP   AC

PAP ISBN-13: 978-0618-54885-9

Manufactured in Singapore
TWP 10 9 8 7 6 5

For Wong's Restaurant, 1951 to 1962,
and Wong's Carryout, 1963 to 1983

Pinky Pig wants a new clarinet,
But she hasn't saved enough money yet.
She works after school from four to seven
Every Friday at Hamburger Heaven.

One day while Pinky is mopping the floor,
She overhears talk by the kitchen door.

"Business had better start picking up fast,
Or next week will have to be Pinky Pig's last."

Pinky heads home nibbling corn on the cob,
Thinking of how to hang on to her job.
"Chef serves the same cheeseburgers day after day.
No wonder the diners have all gone away."

That night Pinky dreams up a plan of attack,
A sure-fire way to bring customers back.

Saturday morning she wolfs breakfast down.
Taking a notebook, she heads straight for town.

Pinky asks shoppers she happens to meet:
"What kind of burgers do you like to eat?"

On Sunday Pinky runs out the back door
To buy supplies from the local art store.

Back home, suggestions are all copied down
In pickle green and burnt burger brown.
Specials are added, with new prices too.
Borders get dressed up in purple and blue.
By the time Ma Pig squeals: "Chow, everyone!"
Hamburger Heaven's new menu is done!

On Monday copies are
turned in to teachers.

Tuesday they're passed out to doctors

. . . and preachers.

Wednesday they pop up in neighborhood stores.

Thursday they're found in
mailboxes and doors.

That night Pinky dreams she plays a duet,
Joined by a cheeseburger on clarinet.

School's out on Friday, and by four o'clock,
Pinky finds diners lined up down the block!

She grabs the new menu to show to the cook.
Chef Rhino gives Pinky a skeptical look.
But when he spots all the diners to feed,
He shoos Pinky out to fetch what he'll need.

Pinky's long list includes gathering leaves,
Plucking red ants off the bark of oak trees,

Filling tin cans with bugs running round,
Digging up worms from under the ground.

She collects acorns, twigs, and pine needles,
Flips over rocks, searching for beetles.

Pinky's back dumping bags on the tables,
Dropping the insects in jars marked with labels:

Caterpillars, Crickets, Cockroaches, Ticks,
Grasshoppers, Ladybugs, and Walking Sticks.
The grill is sizzling and ready to go!
Hamburger patties lined up in a row.

Pinky starts shouting out orders to fill.
Chef Rhino slaps burgers down on the grill.

Burgers with toppings are put on a tray.
DING! goes the bell. Waiters whisk them away.

Porcupine's burger is served on pine needles.
Possum's order comes crawling with beetles.
Mole's is prepared with worms lightly fried.
Aardvark's burger has termites inside.
Burger on acorns; slurp up some slugs;
Burger Deluxe has three kinds of bugs.

Hedgehog loves her
Snailburger Supreme.

Skunk thinks the Stinkbug
Burger's a dream.

Frog's Cricketburger comes out a-chirping.
"B-R-RAAP!" goes Beaver.
"Pardon my burping."

Burger on pine cones, frosted with ants;
Burger cocooned in tropical plants.
Customers leave with crumbs on their faces.
Others scurry to fill empty places.

By six o'clock most have eaten their fill.
A line quickly forms for paying the bill.

"Chef, your burgers are totally awesome!"
Declare Porcupine, Beaver, and Possum.

"Hamburger Heaven's burgers can't be beat!"
Shout happy customers out on the street.

Chef Rhino blushes from all of the praise
And gives Pinky Pig a generous raise.

On the way home Pinky doesn't forget
To stop and pick out that new clarinet.